Me and My Dad

Robin Shaw

Hodder
Children's
Books

We're off down the road,
me and my dad.

There are flowers and birds and sunshine
and houses, but the nicest bit, my
favourite bit, the **BEST** bit's at the end.

There are railings in the alley with a puddle

underneath, so I'll have to be careful in case of...

CROCODILES!

But Dad will save me. "Silly sausage," he'll say.
"Come on you, the best bit's at the end."

Then there's the path
going under the railway,
where trains **R-R-RUMBLE**
and **R-R-ROAR** up above.

It echoes like dinosaurs
going for a stomp.

I could listen all day,
but the best bit's at the end.

There's a house like a castle
with bushes all round.
It *must* have a sleeping princess inside.

She's waiting for a prince to come
and break her *spell*,

but we can't hang about,
because the best bit's at the end.

On the corner, there's Mrs Pot's potted plant shop
with *climbers* and *creepers* filling every window.

I stop by the door to sneak a peek inside, but not

for too long, because the best bit's at the end.

Now there's the pet shop with
the fish tank at the front,

and I wish I was *tiny* and exploring the depths.

I'd dive down deep for treasure until...

Dad says, "Come on little mermaid,
the best bit's at the end."

Next there's the shop with
the old metal bins...

just the right size for a spaceship for me.
I'd take a packed lunch, and blast off
until Dad says...

"TIME TO COME DOWN! THE BEST BIT'S AT THE END."

"Nearly there," says Dad, but there's still just time

to wave "Hello" to the carpets in the window,

and to jump the *cracks* and *gaps* in the pavement. It's a little bit tricky, but we're close to the end.

At last! **HOORAY!**

It's the bookshop café.

It's time for hot chocolate and
for choosing a story

about dinosaurs or spaceships,
princesses or treasure.

Now we can snuggle up
and cuddle up and read.

It's the nicest bit.
It's my favourite bit.
It's the very best bit
at the end.

For Rosie, Heather and Robin

HODDER CHILDREN'S BOOKS

First published in Great Britain in 2017 by Hodder and Stoughton

Text and illustrations © Robin Shaw 2017

The moral rights of the author and illustrator have been asserted.

All rights reserved.

A CIP catalogue record of this book
is available from the British Library.

ISBN: 978 1 444 92811 2

10 9 8 7 6 5 4 3 2 1

Printed and bound in China.

Hodder Children's Books
An imprint of
Hachette Children's Group
Part of Hodder and Stoughton
Carmelite House
50 Victoria Embankment
London EC4Y 0DZ

An Hachette UK Company
www.hachette.co.uk

www.hachettechildrens.co.uk